Pour Out the Rain

Jhana Chambers

ISBN 979-8-89243-873-5 (paperback)
ISBN 979-8-89428-846-8 (hardcover)
ISBN 979-8-89243-874-2 (digital)

Copyright © 2024 by Jhana Chambers

All rights reserved. No part of this publication may be reproduced, distributed, or transmitted in any form or by any means, including photocopying, recording, or other electronic or mechanical methods without the prior written permission of the publisher. For permission requests, solicit the publisher via the address below.

Christian Faith Publishing
832 Park Avenue
Meadville, PA 16335
www.christianfaithpublishing.com

Printed in the United States of America

Dedicated to Jaymes; Imanee; their daughter, Journey; and children who have lost a parent.

Once upon a time, there was a beautiful princess named Imanee. She loved nature and liked to climb the same mountain every day! She would see so many things as she climbed the mountain—birds, insects, different kinds of trees—but her favorite was flowers. Princess Imanee *loved* flowers!

One day, when Princess Imanee was climbing up the mountain, trying to reach the top like she did every day, she saw a man climbing the mountain. This was not normal for the princess to see because she climbed this same mountain every day since she was a little girl, and no one else had ever been seen on the mountain.

The princess said, "Excuse me, but this is my secret climbing spot. How did you find it?"

The man was so amazed by her beauty that he couldn't say anything. He just smiled at the princess.

The princess was confused. She thought to herself, *Why didn't he respond?*

The princess asked him again, "How did you find my secret climbing spot?"

The man smiled and said, "I just so happened to stumble upon it, and I'm glad I did." The man gently took the princess's hand and said, "Hello, beautiful, my name is Prince Jaymes."

The princess blushed.

Talking for only a few seconds led to them talking for hours. The princess learned that Prince Jaymes was from another kingdom in a far-off land and was in town to explore nature and the mountains. The prince loved nature too. He loved hiking, fishing, and anything that was outdoors. Prince Jaymes adored the natural beauty of God's creation. They continued talking nonstop and even climbed to the top of the mountain together.

It started to get dark, so Princess Imanee and Prince Jaymes climbed down the mountain together, and the prince walked the princess home to her castle. The prince asked the princess, "Can I see you again tomorrow?"

The princess said, "Tomorrow, I will be in the Eden Garden from sunrise to sunset. If you are there, then you will see me tomorrow."

Prince Jaymes gently took her hand, kissed it, and said, "Until tomorrow, beautiful."

The next day, Princess Imanee began to walk to the Eden Garden, just as she said. As she entered the garden, she saw Prince Jaymes standing near flowers. As soon as they saw each other, they both smiled and blushed. It was impossible to deny that love was brewing and had started right on that mountain.

They spent all day together in the garden. They both enjoyed nature and the natural beauty in the many things that God created. They talked about everything! Goals, dreams, likes, dislikes—you name it! The prince and princess talked like this as they went on many adventures together over time.

The ultimate adventure was when they got married! The prince and princess were now King Jaymes and Queen Imanee! A little while later, who would have thought that there would be a little princess inside Queen Imanee's belly?

The king and queen were going to have a baby! They were so excited to start their family! Having a kingdom and a family to look after can be a lot of work, but the king and queen enjoyed working hard to take care of their kingdom.

Sadly, even with all their hard work, there are some things that you can't control.

One day, it stopped raining, and it got really hot. The lakes and wells dried up, and there was no water anywhere in the kingdom. The animals and the people started to get sick.

Then the queen got really sick, and it scared the king. Not only was he worried about his wife, but he was worried about the baby in her belly too. The king didn't know what to do. He thought to himself, *I have to take care of my family, and my little princess is the future of our kingdom.*

King Jaymes did what he knew would never fail: he prayed to God.

"Dear God, I need you. There is no water here, and it hasn't rained in months. My queen is in danger, and so is our little princess. My kingdom needs you, but most of all, my family needs you. I know that you will make a way because you always do. Please help me save my family. Amen."

A few days later, no rain had come yet. But the queen started to get better. The king was so happy and thanked God for healing his queen. Shortly after, the king passed away suddenly, and no one knew how or why. The kingdom was very sad, but mostly, the queen was very sad.

The queen loved the king with all her heart. They had planned a lifetime together, and now that was gone.

The last piece she had of King Jaymes was in her belly, their little princess. The next day, after the king passed away, it started raining. It rained so much! All the wells and lakes filled back up. All the people and the animals were able to get as much water as needed, and no one was sick anymore. The kingdom was finally saved!

Although the kingdom was saved, the king was still gone. The queen was still very sad. She thought to herself, *When someone you love is gone, a part of you is gone too, but the love will always be there.* The queen knew God, too, so she decided to pray.

"Dear God, why would you take the king away from me?"

Suddenly, an angel appeared before the queen. The angel said, "Fear not, I am sent by God. Your husband, the king, prayed that God would save his wife, you, the queen. Although God doesn't always answer our prayers the way we want, He does answer them. God has important work for your husband the king to do. He is helping God pour out the rain so that everything and everyone never goes without water again."

The queen cried and said to the angel, "But I miss him so much."

The angel hugged the queen and said, "I know, and that's okay. Remember, this life on earth is temporary, but heaven lasts forever. He is always in your heart, and he will be waiting for you when your time comes and you get to heaven too. Whenever it rains, remember that your husband, the king, is helping God with the rain so you'll never go without water and will keep the flowers that you love growing."

The visit from the angel helped the queen take life one day at a time. Although she will always miss the king, she finds comfort in knowing that she will see him again one day in heaven.

The baby in the queen's belly had grown and grown, and it was finally time for the little princess to arrive. The little princess was finally here! Her name was Princess Journey! The name Journey is a reminder that life is a journey, not a destination, and our true home is heaven.

Queen Imanee loved being a mommy, but she missed King Jaymes every day. As the years went by, the queen would tell Princess Journey about her daddy, King Jaymes. When the princess was old enough, the queen told her all about how God needed Daddy in heaven to help save everyone.

The princess sometimes found it hard to understand why her daddy wasn't here, but she believes in God, too, so she knows that she will see him one day when she is in heaven.

Queen Imanee told Princess Journey, "Whenever it starts to rain, just look up. That's Daddy working with Jesus to water the flowers just for you. When you get ready to go to sleep, say this little prayer and remember God and Daddy are right there."

Princess Journey prayed to God.

"Dear God, when I get to heaven, I can't wait to be with my daddy. I know it's not a visit. Mommy and the Bible says heaven is my true home, and that's where I'll stay. Since you're in heaven with Daddy, can you give him a hug for me? When I get to heaven, I want to be an angel with big wings, helping my daddy pour out the rain."

About the Author

Jhana Chambers was born in Junction City, Kansas. She was raised as a military dependent. Her favorite duty station was Bamberg, Germany, where she met the love of her life, Andre Chambers. She graduated from Le Cordon Bleu College of Culinary Arts in Austin, Texas, in 2011 with honors. She married her husband Andre in June 2012.

Jhana successfully worked as a chef until a car accident forced a career change. She earned her bachelor's degree in the science of nutrition and her master's degree in health education. When she's not working or vacationing with her husband, she is helping others live a healthier lifestyle as a nutritionist, health educator, and health and wellness consultant. *Pour Out the Rain* is her first published book, and she continues to work on other projects that she hopes will be a blessing to the world.

Printed in the USA
CPSIA information can be obtained
at www.ICGtesting.com
LVHW072050161124
796713LV00015B/130